A SUPERPOWER FOR ME

Mariana Llanos

D1402963

Illustrated by Daria Tarawneh

A superpower for me, Mariana Llanos
2015 © Mariana Llanos

©**Mariana Llanos**
For permissions email: mallalocaok@gmail.com

ISBN-13: 978-1515272878

ISBN-10: 1515272877

Illustrations: Daria Tarawneh
Art Design: Mariana Llanos/Julian Galvan

Editing: Sara Dean
          Carol Thompson

Special thanks to Marcela Varela-Sisley for her knowledge about American government.

www.marianallanos.com

To Citizen Aaron and his new superpower

4

My parents look like ordinary people, but I've found out something special about them. We were eating breakfast the other day, when my mom suddenly said,

"Did you know I have a superpower? Can you guess what it is?"

At first, it smelled like a trick question. Moms do that sort of thing.

"You have eyes in the back of your head!" I answered. She probably saw me sneaking a cookie in my backpack.

"No, my superpower is even bigger than that!"

"Wow, can you fly?" Mom's always saying that she's busy as a bee.

"No, but I can tell you that your dad has my same power, too."

That wouldn't be difficult to guess: Dad can fix anything!

"Do you have magic?" I guessed.

"No, silly! If I did it wouldn't take me such a long time to do the laundry."

Then, Mom leaned over and got close to my face. This didn't seem like a trick anymore. Mom had that stony-faced look she has when she tells me to pick up my toys.

"You will have it too, when you turn eighteen."

That's when I knew she was telling the truth.

"W
   h
      a
        t
          ?"
            I cried.

And I fell out of my chair.

"Will I be a super hero? How? What kind?
Will I be able to shoot ice from my hands?

Or turn plants into flying monkeys?
Will I be able to run at the speed of light?"

"Not quite, honey..."

"It would be exciting if I could jump to the clouds! Or if I could breathe underwater... Maybe I could tell the future?"

"No, but your superpower will make our city and country better places to live."

"Will I have the power to build parks? Or cancel school? Maybe I could build a humongous playground downtown.
Will I have a super strength?"

"Oh, you'll have strength alright," Mom said. "Your superpower is one of the most powerful tools any citizen has."

"A tool? If I could choose a super tool, I would pick a magic paintbrush. I would paint pretty rainbows around the city and smiles on sad faces. Oh, I can't wait to tell my friends!"

"Actually, your friends will get the same power when they're eighteen, too."

"HUH?" I scratched my head. "Then why is having a superpower so special?"

All of the sudden my dreams of becoming a sort of super hero didn't seem realistic. "Mom, are you sure you're telling the truth?"

"I'm sure. Do you give up?"

I shrugged my shoulders. I couldn't think of anything else.

"You'll have the power to VOTE! Your vote and your friends' votes will decide what goes on in our city and even our whole country.

Your vote will give you a voice. It will make our government listen to you. As a matter of fact, yesterday I voted to build a new park closer to our house."

"Do you think it will it happen?"

"If enough people vote YES, it will."

"But you only had one vote," I frowned. It didn't sound too powerful to me.

"Honey, one vote can make a difference. Actually, a handful of votes has decided presidential elections in the past."

"Do you mean that I will be able to vote for a president? I'd like to be president someday! I would order people to live in peace and if they say no to me I'd give them cotton candy. Who could say no to cotton candy?"

"I wouldn't," laughed Mom.

"Well, I'll get to work on that," I said, putting on my backpack. "There's an election for class president next month, and I'm going to run for it. I'll give my friends the power to vote for me."

I got up to leave for school, and I gave Mom a kiss. "Thanks for voting to build that park, Mom. You're my hero."

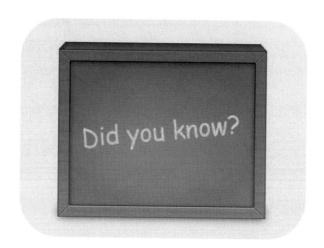

One vote RULES:

In 1867, one vote in Congress decided the purchase of the Alaska Territory... did you know that it was bought from Russia? Even before that, in 1845, one vote in Congress allowed the Republic of Texas to join the United States! Also, in 1876, Rutherford Hayes was elected the nineteenth president of the United States by a one electoral vote difference... ONE vote!

Did you know that our system of government is called a DEMOCRACY? A democracy is when all people have a fair and equal say or vote as to how the government is run. In a democracy, we vote for the people we want to lead our country, like the president, senators, congress, governors, mayor, and much more. The word DEMOCRACY comes from the Greek words 'Demos,' which means people, and 'Kratos,' which means power... so it literally means The Power of the People! Ancient Greeks were the first ones to practice democracy a long, long time ago! **Question:** Can you guess which country has the oldest modern democracy in the world?

Did you know that in the United States we count electoral votes rather than personal votes (popular vote)?

It's true! Each of the fifty states has a given number of Electors who participate in a process called Electoral College. States with more people get more members in their Electoral College. For example, California gets fifty-five electoral votes while Alaska gets only three. When people vote on presidential elections, they're actually voting for an Elector who will represent their vote in Congress. When a candidate for president wins the most electoral votes, at least 270, it means that he or she wins the election! In the 2000 election, one of the closest in history, presidential candidate Al Gore had the most popular votes, but George W. Bush won the most electoral votes... and he became President George W. Bush.

Question: How many electoral votes does your state have?

Did you know that originally only white men were allowed to vote in the United States? My mom wouldn't have liked that! It took several civil rights movements to give African Americans, Native Americans, and women the right to vote. The leaders of these groups, alongside brave activists, often put their own lives and freedom at risk to demand fairness and equality for all. Their demands eventually lead to changes (amendments) in our Constitution: The 15th Amendment allowed male African Americans to vote (1870); the 19th Amendment gave women the vote (1920); the 24th Amendment prohibited any type of payment to vote (1964). Also, the Indian Citizenship Act of 1924 gave Native Americans the right to vote, but some states continued to deny their rights for years to come. The Voting Rights Act was signed by President Johnson in 1965 to ensure that every citizen of the United States was allowed the right to vote.

Question: How would you feel if you were denied the right to vote?

Did you know that every person born in the United States is an American citizen?

This is called 'birthright citizenship'. If your parents are American citizens you are one too, even if you are born in another country. Also, a person can become an American citizen through a process called 'Naturalization.' It's a long process but well worth the wait!

Only American citizens who are at least eighteen years old have the right to vote. Any citizen older than thirty-five years old can become a president, except for those who were naturalized.

Question: Who was the youngest person ever to be elected president of the United States?

Find more

SUPERBOOKS by Mariana Llanos:

Tristan Wolf
Spanish: Tristán Lobo

A Planet for Tristan Wolf

The Wanting Monster

Spanish: El Monstruo Quierelotodo

No Birthday for Mara

Spanish: Mara sin Cumpleaños

The Staircase on Pine Street

www.amazon.com
www.marianallanos.com

Made in the USA
San Bernardino, CA
18 November 2015